RAINBOW FISH
SPIKE AND THE SUBSTITUTE

Text by Leslie Goldman

Illustrations by Benrei Huang

HarperFestival®
A Division of HarperCollinsPublishers

Spike and Rainbow Fish

raced to school.

Today was the best day

of the week.

It was show-and-tell day.

All the fish in Miss Cuttle's class
loved show-and-tell.
It was a chance to share their
treasures with their friends.

Spike could not wait.

He had found something

extra-special to show his friends.

It was a piece of coral

shaped like a fish.

7

"Attention!" Miss Cuttle called.
"It is time to settle down
and start our day."
Everyone did.

Spike did his best to listen.
But all he could think about
was his great piece of coral.
He just could not wait
to show it off.

Quietly, Spike picked up

his piece of coral

and showed it to Rainbow Fish.

Soon, the two little fish forgot

all about Miss Cuttle's lesson.

"Spike," said Miss Cuttle,

"please put that away.

We have work to do."

Spike quickly put the coral away.

Paying attention was not easy.
Spike could not resist
taking out the coral again.
"Spike, you will have to wait for
show-and-tell like everyone else,"
Miss Cuttle said.

"You better be careful,"
said Rainbow Fish.
"Miss Cuttle only gives three
chances. You do not want
your coral to end up in the
treasure chest."

Spike knew this was true.

But, just before recess,

Spike thought to himself,

Miss Cuttle will not mind if I

take a quick look at my coral.

But Miss Cuttle did mind.

"Spike, you know the rules.

This is the third time that I have

asked you to put that away.

Now your treasure goes

in the treasure chest."

The rest of the day passed

very slowly for Spike.

He listened to the other students

talk about their treasures.

Spike wanted his coral back.

He was not sad. He was mad.

Later, Spike told Rainbow Fish,

"Miss Cuttle is mean.

That was not fair.

I wish she was not our teacher."

"Be careful what you wish for,"

warned Rainbow Fish.

The next morning Spike found
Mrs. Crabbitz in their cave classroom.
All the fish began to talk at once.

"Why is Mrs. Crabbitz here?"

asked Rosie.

"Where is Miss Cuttle?"

Rainbow Fish asked.

19

Mrs. Crabbitz cleared her throat.

"Settle down! Settle down!

Miss Cuttle is out sick.

I will be your teacher today.

I expect you all to behave,"

she said.

Everyone was sad that
Miss Cuttle was sick.
Everyone but Spike.

Mrs. Crabbitz quickly got the class
settled down and ready for work.
But she wasn't like Miss Cuttle.
Mrs. Crabbitz was very strict.

Mrs. Crabbitz yelled all day long.

School was not much fun

without Miss Cuttle.

The class missed their teacher.

Spike began to miss his teacher, too.

He wondered if Miss Cuttle

had stayed home because

he had misbehaved.

The more Spike thought about it,

the worse he felt.

When the class lined up for recess,

Spike was so upset that he swam

into a corner by himself.

"I am *not* going," he said.

"You cannot make me!"

"If you want to be alone,
that is fine. But you still
have to come outside,"
said Mrs. Crabbitz.

26

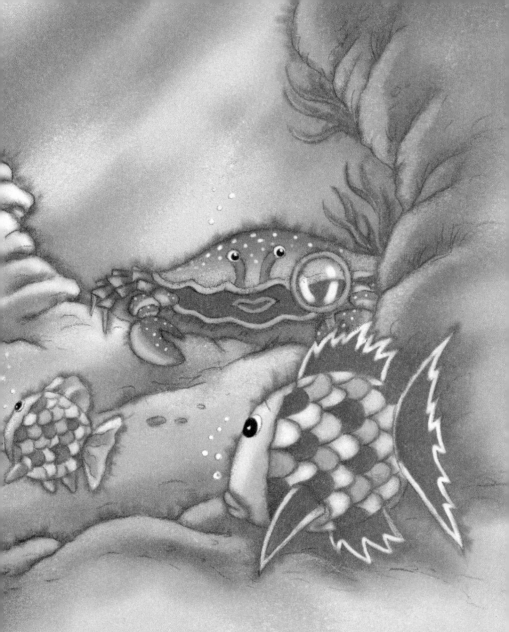

Spike knew he had to listen to
Mrs. Crabbitz, so he followed her
out to the Shipwreck.

"You can build a
sculpture while you are
all by yourself over here,"
said Mrs. Crabbitz as she gathered
rocks, shells, and seaweed.

"When I need time to think,

I build sculptures,"

said Mrs. Crabbitz.

Her pile quickly turned

into a beautiful sculpture.

Spike decided to make his own.

The rest of the day

passed quickly for Spike.

At the end of the lessons,

Spike stayed behind.

He told Mrs. Crabbitz

he was sorry for misbehaving.

The next morning,

Spike was happy to see

Miss Cuttle back at school.

Only one thing worried him:

Did Mrs. Crabbitz tell

her that he had misbehaved?

Miss Cuttle swam over to Spike
and said, "Mrs. Crabbitz told
me about your sculpture!
Would you like to share it at
show-and-tell?"

"You bet!" said Spike.

"I knew you would miss Miss
Cuttle," Rainbow Fish said.